Diary o

Book One

Peter Patrick

William Thomas

What happens on the mission, stays on the mission...

Diary of a Super Spy (Book 1)

Peter Patrick, William Thomas

Also in the Diary of a Super Spy series:

For Ethan, Chelsea and Sophie.

Diary of a Super Spy

Peter Patrick

William Thomas

Chapter 1

Tuesday Morning:

Zombies in the Classroom

Oh, come on!

Not another substitute teacher?

Miss Jackson was away all last week, and now we have another substitute teacher. Hopefully, this one is better than the last one. Mr. Greyson, last week's teacher, had to go to the hospital because in gym class, Jack the Jock kicked a soccer ball in his... well, he kicked it into an area of the body that hurts a lot.

My name is Charlie Chucky, and I am in the sixth grade. I am the son of an International Super Spy who works for an agency so secret that even my Dad doesn't know the name of it.

My Super Spy Dad has had dinner with the President, talked with aliens from Jupiter, and swapped phone numbers with a very intelligent gorilla. His life is *super* exciting.

My life is not that exciting. I go to school, dream about talking to the prettiest girl in the school, Mia, and come home again. I'm not popular – far from it – but I have my best friend, Harley, who I spend a lot of time with.

This is me.

And this is my friend, Harley.

As you can see, we are not the coolest kids in school.

"Hi, Charlie. Today is going to be a great day," Harley whispers to me as I take a seat in class. "Tuesday's are always great, but today is going to be extra great."

"Why do you say that?" I ask.

"Miss Jackson is away again today, and we've got another substitute teacher. How cool is that? We can do whatever we want today! Plus, we don't have to put up with Miss Jackson's sneezing."

Miss Jackson has the loudest sneeze in the world.

Last week when she had the flu, she was sneezing every three minutes. Her sneeze was so loud that everybody in the class had to wear ear plugs. One time she sneezed, and the ground shook so much that trees started falling over and birds fell out of the sky. It was totally crazy.

"I love substitute teachers Harley, but this new substitute teacher doesn't look very smart. She doesn't even look like she can teach a class," I comment on our new teacher. "Have we had her before?"

"Nope. I think she's a real newbie. I haven't even seen her around the school before. I'm not even sure that she has taught children previously."

"Really?" I question.

"Yep. When I walked into the classroom this morning, she asked what do we do all day. She had no idea what we do in class. And when I told her, she looked really confused and had to write lots and lots of notes. She really had no idea what we do all day."

Harley is a good kid. He is always the first to arrive in class and the last one to leave. He knows all the teachers and is always helping them in his lunch break.

"And what did you tell her?"

"I told her that we do math first, then spelling, then history and then more math, if we have time. I told her that we love lots and lots of work because it helps us succeed in our tests."

"Oh no," I say to Harley. "You should have told her that we play computer games first, then computer games, and then more computer games!"

I like computer games.

"Oh yeah," Harley says. "That's a really good idea, Charlie. I'll try that tomorrow. But I'll tell her that we do math first, and then computer games."

"Aw, man," I shake my head. "Did your Dad come home from his science trip yesterday?"

"He came back last night, but he smelt like poo. I could smell him as he walked up the street. It was so bad that even the dog wouldn't go near him."

"Yuk!"

Harley's Dad is one of the world's best scientists. At the moment, he is studying if the poo of an African Mountain Gorilla can help your skin become stronger.

He thinks the more African Mountain Gorilla poo you rub on your skin, the healthier it becomes! He thinks that his skin will become so strong that he won't have to worry about wearing clothes in future.

Scientists study the weirdest stuff.

"What about your Dad? Did he come back last night?" Harley asks me.

"Yep. He came back from fighting a water monster in the Amazon rainforest," I explain to Harley. Harley is the only other kid that knows my Dad is an International Super Spy. "The monster tried to eat all the trees in the Amazon rainforest, so my Dad had to stop him. He traveled over to Brazil, walked for three days through the ultra-thick jungle, and then came face to face with a twelve-foot water monster."

"Wow! How did he stop him?"

"He just asked him to stop eating all the trees."

"Is that it?"

"Dad said 'Excuse me, Mr. Water Monster, can you please stop eating all the trees in the Amazon rainforest?', and the monster said, 'Sure. No problem.' And then he walked away!"

"Whoa. That sounds totally easy. Even I could do that. Being a Super Spy must be so cool."

"I'll be a Super Spy one day, Harley," I say. "I can take you on my adventures with me."

"You? A Super Spy?" Harley laughs. "How could you be a Super Spy? You struggle to tie up your shoelaces each morning!"

That's true. It's not that I can't tie up my shoelaces, but I get distracted each time I try. Yesterday, I tied up my shoelaces while watching television, but I tied them to the couch. I didn't walk very far before falling flat on my face.

"Quiet!" the new substitute teacher yells from the front of the classroom. "I need everyone to listen to me. I am going to teach you about... um... things... and... um... stuff. So listen to me! I am the teacher, and I don't want anyone else to talk for the rest of the day. Understand?"

Harley and I raise our eyebrows at each other. This is going to be a fun day.

The whole class waits for the teacher to continue, but she doesn't say anything else. She just stares at us for the next five minutes while licking her lips.

That's really strange.

"Excuse me, Miss?" I eventually say. "Can we please play some games?"

"Hmmm..." the substitute teacher says as she stares at me. "Yes, of course. We can play games for yummy children."

"Yummy?" I ask.

"Oh no," she says. "I didn't mean yummy... I meant... um... yellow."

"Yellow? That doesn't even make sense," I whisper.

There is something strange about our substitute teacher, and I can't quite put my finger on it.

Maybe it's her hair?

"But let me introduce myself first," she finally states in a croaky voice. "My name is Miss Zomb. Pleased to eat… er, meet you."

For some reason, she has crossed out the last two letters of her name on the blackboard, and she smells funny too.

I might not be the smartest kid in class, but I am already suspicious of this lady…

Chapter 2

Tuesday Afternoon

Hanging with my Super Spy Dad

Ka-zap!

My Super Spy Dad fires a shot of his newest piece of work equipment – a super small, super powerful, laser gun.

One of the bonuses of having a Super Spy Dad is that he brings home all the latest equipment from the Super Spy agency, and I get to try all the new gadgets. At the Super Spy agency, they have the world's best gadget scientist developing the world's best inventions.

Just last week, I tried his new time machine.

It didn't work very well, so we were stuck going back five seconds at a time. It was a bit silly really – as soon as we went back in time, we saw ourselves going into the time machine.

So we tried again – and then we saw ourselves watching ourselves going into the time machine.

So we tried again – and then we saw ourselves watching ourselves watching ourselves going into the time machine.

"This is a mega-powerful, ultra-strong gun, Charlie. It can never fall into the hands of the wrong person, or things will be terrible. This gun is so strong that it will even freeze the scariest of scary bad guys," Dad smiles. "There is not a person in the world that can resist the powers of this gun. It freezes anything that you shoot into a ball of ice."

"Whoa. That's totally cool, Dad. I love it. What are you going to use it for?"

"I will use it on anything that won't co-operate with me. Or maybe I'll just use it on a hot day to freeze the house. That way, we won't have to use the air-conditioner."

"Good idea, Dad," I say. "But that gun looks very familiar. Actually, it looks a lot like your last gun. Do you remember that gun?"

"Um... yes. I remember that gun Charlie, but I thought we agreed that we wouldn't mention that gun again."

"Oops. Sorry, Dad. I forgot. I won't say anything else about it."

When Dad brought home his last new gun, he accidentally shot a hole in our floor.

The problem was that it was the most powerful gun ever built.

That hole went straight through the floor and all the way to the other side of the world. We could even wave to the people on the other side of the hole.

We spent months filling that back in. And Mom was so unhappy with Dad that we agreed we wouldn't speak about it again.

"What case are you working on now, Dad?" I change the conversation.

"We're working on a big case right now, son. It's extremely dangerous and very creepy. This case is like a horror movie, but it's real life. It is one of the most intense cases I have ever worked on, and it even scares me a little. And you know how hard it is to scare me."

"Except for when you are watching children's movies."

"And we weren't going to talk about that either," Dad says, shaking his head.

My Dad is the worst person in the world to watch a movie with. Even films made for babies scare him. And he cries at the end of every movie!

It is so embarrassing.

"What is the case about, Dad?" I ask, very interested. "Is there anything that I can do to help you with it? I would love to help you with the case."

"I'm afraid I can't let you help with this case, Charlie. It is too dangerous for someone like you. We have our best spies working on the case right now and they are trying to stop this threat. We have even bought in the German, Australian, and Japanese Super Spies to help us solve this case."

"So what is so scary that I can't help you with?"

"I'll tell you, Charlie, but you have to promise to keep this very quiet."

"I promise."

"Ok. We have information that there are zombies trying to attack our great country!"

"Zombies?!"

"Yes, son, zombies. But not just any sort of dumb zombies. Nope. This is a new breed of zombies that talk, walk, and think. We don't know where they have come from, but they are scarier than anything you could ever imagine. If you think about the scariest thing that you can, double that, and then double that again. That is what we are talking about."

"Whoa, that's totally scary, Dad."

"And these new zombies aren't like the last lot of zombies that tried to attack our nation. Those zombies were slow, stupid, and dumb. We didn't need our best spies because they were very easy to defeat. When the zombies attacked last year, all they wanted to attack was the fast food store."

"Why did they attack a fast food store?"

"Because they were hungry. When we got there, we found that all they wanted was hamburgers. They didn't want to hurt anyone, they just wanted five hamburgers each. So we offered them all the hamburgers they could eat, as long as they stayed locked up in our prison. They agreed."

"Being a Super Spy sounds pretty easy sometimes, Dad."

"Sometimes it is easy, Charlie. But not this time. No way. This new breed of zombies is going to be very hard to defeat. We have our very best zombie experts trying to build a profile of the zombies so that we can predict their movements. If we know where they are going, then we can stop them. But it is really hard because they are so different to the ones that attacked last year. The new zombies don't want to eat hamburgers."

"What do they want to eat?"

"We're not sure yet. We are trying to work that out. Our zombie locator machine is tracking them at the moment, and as soon as we can find them, we will capture them. But they are not dumb. They are smart zombies, and that is what makes them so dangerous."

"Is there anything else different about these zombies?"

"They are bigger, quicker, and smarter. And they smell really bad. And they're very good at disguises too."

"What sort of disguises?" I ask.

I instantly think of my new substitute teacher.

"This breed of zombies has been known to dress up as things you wouldn't expect zombies to dress up as. We've heard that they have dressed up as bus drivers, trees, and even crocodiles. They are very, very sneaky."

"Crocodiles? That's crazy."

"Charlie, if the zombies attack, I want you to hide. Do you know where the best place to hide from a zombie is?" Dad smiles.

"No. Where?"

"In the 'living' room!" Dad laughs. "Get it? Ha! The 'living' room. Because the zombies are dead! And 'living' is opposite to dead. Get it?"

"That's a bad joke, Dad," I shake my head.

My Dad loves to tell bad jokes.

Every time we go to the grocery store to buy milk, the cashier asks Dad if he would like the milk in a bag, and he always replies, 'No. Just leave it in the carton!'

Sigh.

"Do you know why the zombies fell asleep?" Dad is still laughing.

"Dad. Stop," I groan. "I don't want to hear any more of your bad jokes. Just stop."

"They fell asleep because they were 'dead' tired! Haha! Get it, Charlie?" Dad laughs loudly. "Dead tired!"

"I get it, Dad," I shake my head again. "But Dad, could these zombies be dressed as school teachers?"

"Don't be ridiculous, Charlie. I said that they dress up as all sorts of things, but they definitely wouldn't dress up as school teachers. I couldn't see why a zombie would want to dress up as a school teacher. That would be a really absurd costume for a zombie. I couldn't imagine that happening. Nope. No chance. Never."

"But my 6th grade teacher..."

"Don't be so silly, Charlie. Zombies don't want to play at school. They wouldn't be interested in staying there. They have more important things to do, like take over the world. This new breed of zombies is not going to waste their time hanging around at places like your school. That's a very silly idea, Charlie."

"But Dad-"

"No, son. These zombies are interested in smelly, sweaty little people that are about half the size of an average human. They're not interested in school children. They want to find something to eat, they don't want to learn math. Why would a zombie need to know math? And can you imagine that? A zombie in the classroom. Maybe they would start school at 'ate' o'clock! Ha! I'm so funny. Get it, Charlie? 'Ate' o'clock, instead of 'eight' o'clock. Haha!"

Groan.

Dad is one of the smartest people I have ever met – but he can be so dumb.

I know that sounds strange, but he is.

He seems to know everything about everything - but then he can't even see the glasses that sit on his face.

He'll ask Mom over and over again where his glasses are, but they are always on his head!

"Can I have a turn with the new gun?" I change the conversation before Dad can tell me any more zombie jokes.

"Sure Charlie, you can try my new gun," Dad hands me the new gadget. "But you need to be extra careful with this weapon. This gun is super powerful and can do all sorts of damage if you shoot it in the wrong direction. We don't want to hurt anything."

"Yes, Dad," I reply. "How does it work?"

"Our gadget scientist designed it to be really simple, Charlie. You just point it at the target and shoot. That's all there is to it."

The laser gun is really light, and fun to swing around. I pretend to shoot things, jumping into my best shooting pose.

"Ka-zap, ka-zap!" I shout as I pretend to shoot the gun.

But then, my finger slips...

Ka-zap!

I fire the gun into the yard, but the neighbor's cat steps into my shot!

Oops.

"Well," Dad scratches his head, looking at the cat. "This could be a problem, Charlie. It seems that you have shot the cat and frozen her into a solid ball of ice."

"Sorry Dad," I apologize. "I didn't mean to do it. My finger slipped on the trigger. Sorry."

"Um… we'll have to melt the cat out of the ice. And we'll have to do it quick, before our neighbor gets home. Charlie, go and get your mother's hairdryer. That might just work."

I slip the gun into my backpack, and race off to get Mom's hairdryer. Actually, I wouldn't mind if the neighbor's cat stays frozen – she always steals my underwear off the washing line and then runs around the neighborhood with my jocks over her head.

It is so embarrassing! But luckily for the cat, Dad is able to melt her back into the land of the living.

Chapter 3

Wednesday Morning

Return to Zombie School

As I walk into school on Wednesday morning, I notice kids running around everywhere.

Everyone seems crazy, and they are all breaking the rules. Our school is usually like a zoo, but this morning, it is more like a wildlife safari range.

There are students climbing walls, kids dancing the salsa down the corridors, and even children discussing the finer details of philosophy in the yard.

Something strange is going on this morning, and I have no idea what it is.

I go to investigate what is happening, but then I see the craziest sight of all...

My friend Harley is breaking the rules!

What is going on in this place?

Harley is sprinting at full pace, and smiling happily. He is really enjoying running up the hallway.

Harley is built like a brick – short, wide, and strong.

To see Harley run is strange enough, but to see Harley run up the hallway, where it is forbidden, is outrageous.

Harley loves the rules.

He loves the rules so much that he has a poster on the wall of his bedroom with the school rules written on them.

On top of that list is *'No running in the halls at school,'* followed by *'No climbing on the roof when wearing an alien costume.'*

They had to make that second rule because my classmate Terrance is convinced that he is an alien.

He always climbs the roof at school and tries to talk to his alien friends.

I think he even has a UFO in his backyard.

Teachers make the craziest rules – like what is wrong with running in the hall anyway?

We are capable people - it's not like we are going to trip and hurt anyone.

But as that thought goes through my mind, Harley's foot hits a crack in the ground...

Harley is a solid boy, and when he lands, anything in his way goes flying!

TRIP!

Crash!

Harley knocks over a group of four girls as he tumbles down the hall.

I guess that is why we're not allowed to run inside.

"Wow," I say to Harley as I help him up. "That fall must have hurt. You took quite a tumble, Harley."

"Oops," Harley mumbles. "I'm really sorry everyone. I don't usually run so fast. My foot hit a crack, and I tripped. I'm sorry!"

"Why were you running in the hall anyway?" I ask. "You know that it is against the rules to run inside the building. It's the first rule of the school. It's what we are told every single day by the teachers – *'No running in the halls at school.'*"

"I know the school rules, Charlie," he says. "I have memorized all 240 of them. I can tell you all of them, if you would like."

"No thanks. But what were you doing?"

"I was breaking the school rules," he grins.

"Why? I don't think I have ever seen you break the school rules."

"Because there are no teachers at school today," Harley says. "There is nobody here to tell us off for breaking the rules. We can do whatever we want, Charlie. Whatever we want. The rules don't matter today."

"What do you mean there are no teachers? There must be some teachers here. School is about to start, and we can't have school without teachers."

"There are some teachers – but they're all substitute teachers!"

"*All* the teachers are substitute teachers?"

"Even the Principal."

"Really?" I question.

It seems quite unusual for all the teachers to be away from school on the same day. Something weird is definitely happening.

"What happened to all the other normal teachers? Miss Jackson, Mr. U. Lose, Mrs. I. P. Daily, or Mr. G. Whiz? None of them are at school today?"

"Not one regular teacher is here today. I've checked every classroom, and the staffroom. I'm telling you that they are all substitute teachers."

"Don't you think that's a bit strange?"

"Maybe," Harley shrugs. "But so are farts. Think about that, Charlie. They are the expulsion of 59% nitrogen, 21% hydrogen, 9% carbon dioxide, 7% methane, and 4% oxygen out of your body. Weird."

"A little off topic there, Harley," I shake my head. "So, where are all the normal teachers?"

"They've all disappeared. Nobody knows where they are. But who cares? Without all the normal teachers, we can break all the rules! We can even eat in our classroom. Did you hear me, Charlie? We can eat in our classroom!"

"Yep. Really going wild there, Harley," I groan sarcastically.

Harley laughs loudly while grabbing his sandwich, and walking into our classroom, "Woo! Look at me! I'm eating in the classroom! Woo!"

"Wait, Harley," I stop him. "Are you sure they are *all* substitute teachers?"

"It sure is true."

"Then where are all the substitute teachers? Why are there no teachers in the classrooms?"

"I heard one of them say that they are going to a meeting in the staffroom before the whole school assembly this morning. You can go and check for yourself. They are all going to be in the staffroom."

"Do you want to come with me?"

"No way. I have a sandwich to eat. In. The. Classroom!"

"Harley, I think something strange is going on here," I say. "I don't think all the teachers are sick. I think they have been kidnapped!"

"Don't be so silly, Charlie," Harley says. "There is nothing strange going on. You worry too much, Charlie. Stop worrying and just enjoy today for what it is – a day of total freedom at school!"

"No, Harley. I think it's worse than that. And I'm going to find out what has happened!"

Chapter 4

Wednesday School Time

Substitute Teachers Meeting

Cautiously, I walk through the halls of our school, checking each classroom as I go.

I look into Mrs. Brown's class.

The class is currently having a huge food fight with pies, cream, and hotdogs – yep, definitely no teacher there!

I check Mr. Graham's art class – they are currently painting their self-portraits…

On the walls!

No teacher in there either.

And Miss Homer's high-achievement math class… well, they are still studying math, even though there is no teacher. They love math. Last year, when the school was closed because of a snowstorm, they still came to school. But the school wasn't open – so they studied math outside in the middle of a blizzard!

Looking into Mr. Nelson's 6th grade class, I see a soccer game happening – but they are using a backpack for the soccer ball!

Mia, the prettiest girl in school, is playing the game. Mia is so nice and friendly, and loves to play sports.

"Um, hi," I blush when she sees me staring at her.

"Hi Charlie," she smiles sweetly as she hard-core kicks the backpack across the room. "How cool is this? There are no real teachers today. This is so awesome. We get to do whatever we want in school."

"It's cool, I suppose."

"What are you doing?" she asks.

"Um... nothing."

"Cool. Do you want to kick the ball with us?"

"Um, I don't think so."

"Come on. It's fun kicking a backpack soccer ball in the classroom!"

"I would like to, but I have to go and have a look at something. I really need to figure this problem out."

"What could be more important than having fun, Charlie?" Mia asks.

"Nothing," I shrug.

"Then where are you going?"

"I'm going to see where all the substitute teachers are and check what they are doing. I think something might be wrong with the real teachers," I say nervously.

"Why?"

"Don't you think it's weird that *all* the teachers are missing from school on the same day?"

"I suppose," Mia shrugs. "It's strange, but we should enjoy the moment. Things like this only happen once during our time at school, and we have to make sure that we take advantage of it. Don't get all stressed out, just enjoy today. You've got to live in the moment, Charlie. YOLO!"

"Yolo," I sigh in response.

Nobody else thinks that something strange is happening. I am going to have to figure this out myself.

"Don't leave, Charlie. You should stay here with me," Mia says as I walk away from her classroom.

"Something strange is happening today Mia, and I'm going to find out what it is."

"Ok," she smiles. "If anything goes wrong, you make sure you save us, Charlie. You can be our hero! Hero Charlie!"

Her entire class laughs at me.

"Hero Charlie!" I hear them shout as I walk away from the class. "Save us!"

Oh man.

It's bad enough that the school has gone crazy, but now Mia also thinks I'm a guy who worries about things too much!

Today is not going well.

Slowly, I make my way through the rest of the crazy kids in the halls, and finally, make it to the entrance of the staffroom.

As I walk to the staffroom door, I hear the murmur of teachers chatting, but they sound a lot different to normal teachers.

They sound more evil.

Their voices are creepier and spookier than I have ever heard. And we have some frightening teachers at school.

Like our science teacher, Mr. Scary. He's totally scary.

He likes to hide under the desks in our classrooms, and then jump out wearing a ghost mask when we are halfway through a test.

He scares everyone.

I poke my head in the door of the staff room to look at all the substitute teachers. They are all huddled together, and they all look a little bit strange.

And wow – they smell bad too!

Miss Zomb, my substitute teacher, stands at the front of the room with a notepad and pencil. She scribbles three things on the notepad and then calls out to the other teachers.

"It is all going to plan," Miss Zomb tells the other teachers. "Steps one and two have been completed. Step one: all the real teachers have been captured, and step two: we have replaced them as substitute teachers. Now it is up to us to complete step three."

"What is step three again?" one of the teachers asks.

"Step three: capture all the children. With all the real teachers gone, there is nobody here to stop us. We will capture all the children this morning at the school assembly. Because there are no real teachers left, it leaves all the children to us. We are free to do what we want with them."

"What if the children fight back?" another teacher asks her.

"They won't," Miss Zomb replies. "We have planned this perfectly. We will trick the children into the situation so that by the time they realize what has happened, it will be too late! It will all happen so quickly that they won't have a chance to fight back."

"But what if someone else tries to stop us?"

"Nobody can stop us! We are too clever, too slick, and too fast!" Miss Zomb laughs. "We have outsmarted everyone! By the end of today, all the children will be ours, and then we can move onto the next school for more yummy children!"

"Hmmm… yummy children," one of them says. "Yum, yum, yum. Yum, yum, yum."

"I can't wait for the yummy assembly," another mentions. "We will get all the children in one spot. Hmmm… it's eating time!"

"Yes... eating time. I love eating children. Especially the little ones," another groans. "Ahhh... yum. The little ones. The little ones are the tastiest!"

All the substitute teachers in the room laugh, but then one of the wigs fall off!

What is happening?

This seems like a planned attack on all the schools in our town!

"Yummy children?" I whisper to myself so they can't hear me. "Wait a minute... They are not teachers... They're all zombies! And they are going to eat us all!"

"What's happening in there?" Harley whispers over my shoulder.

"Harley? What are you doing here? I thought you were busy eating a sandwich in the classroom?" I ask.

"I *was* eating a sandwich in the classroom! But I finished it. And I tell you, Charlie, that was the best sandwich I have ever eaten. Can you believe it? I ate a sandwich in the classroom! I'm so wild!"

"You are so crazy," I say sarcastically. "But we have a big problem, Harley."

"What is it?"

"The teachers are all zombies!"

"Zombies?!" Harley is surprised. "Are you sure? How can you tell?"

"My Dad said that there was a group of intelligent zombies ready to attack our town, and I am sure that this is them. And the worst bit is, they are planning to kidnap all the kids in our school!"

"How?"

"I don't know, but they are planning to do it this morning in the school assembly!"

"Excuse me!" a zombie teacher says to us!

Oh no!

They have heard us!

"Do not move, little children," another zombie teacher says. "You need to come with us."

Two zombie teachers stand next to us - one with his hand on Harley's shoulder!

"Quick, Harley, run!" I shout.

Quickly, I race away from the staffroom, but a substitute teacher chases me!

I don't want to get caught by this zombie teacher!

My heart is pounding as I race down the hallway with my bag!

I'm running as fast as my legs will go!

The teacher is following me, and he is fast for a teacher!

And really fast for a zombie teacher!

Oh no!

I look over my shoulder and see Harley still next to the staffroom door. He has been stopped by the other zombie teacher!

Agh! My friend has been captured!

"Hmmm… yummy children," the zombie teacher says again. "Come back! Come back!"

No!

This is bad.

Very bad!

I race into an empty classroom, jump out the open window, and then run along the yard until I reach the hall entrance again. As I look over my shoulder, I see the teacher climbing out the window!

Teachers aren't supposed to do that!

Back inside the hall, I look for somewhere to hide!

I jump into one of the hall closets, and lock the door shut behind me.

Quietly, I wait to see if the teacher has followed me…

I can smell the teacher as soon as he walks into the hallway!

Oh man, he smells bad!

And he must be getting closer because the smell is getting stronger!

I hide deeper into the closet and hold my breath, hoping he doesn't hear me breathing.

But as soon as I am hiding under one of the shelves, I hear the door start to shake!

He is trying to come in!

No!

What am I going to do? I don't have anything to defend myself with.

This is very bad!

Crunch!

The zombie teacher breaks the lock on the door!

I'm terrified!

A zombie teacher is about to catch me!

"Come here, little child," he mumbles. "I just want to talk to you. That's what teachers do, they talk to children. Let's talk, little child. Come here. Come here."

I hide under a shelf, hoping that he can't reach me.

"There you are," I hear him say. "Don't be afraid, little child. I'm not scary. I just want to talk about what you saw in the staffroom."

"No way," I reply. "You said that you wanted to eat all the children!"

"Don't be so silly. What a silly thing to say. Teachers don't eat children. Come here, and I promise I won't eat you, little child."

Slowly, I creep out from under the shelf, but the zombie teacher moves towards me with his hands outstretched...

"You look so yummy!" he says. "Come here, yummy child!"

"Ahh!" I scream. "Get away!"

As the teacher's arms reach out to grab me - his pants fall down!

In the second that it takes for him to look at his pants, I race past him, and back down the hallway!

"Nooo!" I hear him yell after me. "Come back, tasty little child!"

Quickly, I am out of his reach.

I race down two different hallways before I turn around and check behind me.

There is nothing behind me.

Good.

The creepy zombie teacher isn't following me anymore.

He must be too busy trying to find a belt.

With my heart still beating very hard, I sneak into one of the empty classrooms and grab my cell phone.

I'll call my Super Spy Dad.

He'll know exactly what to do.

"Hello?" Dad answers the phone.

"Dad!" I yell down the phone. "The zombies-"

"Yes, Charlie. We are still chasing the zombies, but it's a big job. It's going to take a long time to track down the zombies. We've been able to locate some information that would suggest that they are very active at the moment. They seem to be somewhere in our city, but we are unsure where they are at the moment. It's a very complex case to work on. We know they are here but finding the zombies is certainly the most difficult part of the case. But don't worry, we are working on locating them now."

"I know, Dad! They're-"

"They're scary. That's right, Charlie. They are very scary. If you see them, make sure you let me know. But don't go near them, they are very dangerous. Make sure you call me straight away if you see any zombies. Straight away. No messing about. I want you to pick up the phone and call me if you see anything suspicious. I want to know right away if anyone sees a zombie."

"But Dad! You don't understand. Listen to me! The zombies-"

"Yes, yes, Charlie. The zombies are quite scary. And remember Charlie, they are very good at disguises. So make sure that you keep your eyes open, and tell me if you see anything that might be suspicious. These zombies are very clever and could be dressed up as anything. You never know when you might come across one of these zombies. They could be hiding anywhere or could be dressed up as anything. They could even be dressed up as the gardener at your school. If you see anything suspicious, call me straight away."

"But Dad, I've seen scary-"

"Mary? Who is Mary?" Dad interrupts.

"What?"

"You said you've seen Mary."

"I didn't say that."

"You just said it then. You said that you've seen Mary."

"No! I said that I've seen scary-"

"Hairy? Who is hairy?"

"No - scary!"

"Fairy?"

"Scary!"

"Perry?"

"Scary!!"

"Merry?"

"Scary!!" I shout down the phone. Dad doesn't have the best hearing.

"Oh, scary. Yes, yes. The zombies are very scary. I have told you that. There is no doubt about that. They are some of the scariest enemies we have encountered. But don't worry, we are working really hard on the case right now. We will find them."

"But Dad!"

"Isn't it school time right now, Charlie? Shouldn't you be in class now?"

"Yes. But Dad-"

"No buts, Charlie. School is very important. You should always study very hard at school. It's important to learn all that you can at school because it will help you later in life. And not just study. You should also listen at school. You have to listen to your teachers. Listening is a very important skill. If you don't listen to people, you might miss some vital information. Remember to listen, Charlie."

"But Dad-"

"Don't worry about the zombies, Charlie. I will find them sooner or later. That's my job as an international Super Spy, and I am very good at it. We have our best spies working on this case. But you shouldn't miss lessons. You need to go back into your classroom now, Charlie."

"But Dad!"

"No, son. Get off the phone and get back to class. School is important."

"Ugh!"

I hang up the phone.

My Super Spy Dad is no help at all!

The school is in danger from a zombie attack, my friend Harley is in massive trouble, and my Dad won't listen to me!

This is bad.

I thought that having a daily math test was bad, but this is so much worse.

The zombie teachers are going to complete step three of their plan and capture all the kids in my school. I can't let the zombie teachers take over my school and eat all the students.

I cannot let that happen!

I have to stop the zombie teachers before the school assembly this morning!

There is only one thing left to do...

It is up to me to save the school.

But how?

How can I stop all those zombies?

Then I remember that I still have Dad's new laser gun in my backpack...

Chapter 5

Wednesday School Assembly

Defending the School!

I race to the school gym, but by the time I have made it, the weekly assembly has already started.

All the kids in our school are sitting in the gym, waiting for the substitute teachers to begin talking. They look so excited, but they don't know what is about to happen!

Harley is standing next to a zombie teacher, and the teacher has his hand on him. Harley looks like he hasn't been hurt... yet.

I hide behind the gym door and try to listen to the zombie teachers talk with each other.

Oh man, they smell bad!

My eyes are almost watering with the bad stink.

"We are ready," Miss Zomb says to another teacher. "All the children have now gathered in the gym, and our plan is almost complete. Nothing can stop us now."

"Nothing can stop us," the other teacher laughs. "Our plan is perfect."

The zombie teachers laugh with each other as they walk around the gym.

This is so bad.

The zombie teachers look so mean and scary – I'm not sure if I can defeat them. Maybe Harley can help me?

"Harley," I quietly try to get my friends attention. I have to be quiet, so the zombie teachers don't hear me. "Harley."

But Harley doesn't respond!

Standing next to the zombie teacher, he reaches inside his backpack. Maybe he is going to get something to help me...

Oh no.

Harley pulls out another sandwich and starts eating it in the gym. He knows that 'No eating in the gym' is school rule number 38.

Wow, he is really going wild breaking the rules today.

I look at all the zombie teachers, and they are all drooling and licking their lips as they stare at the students. This is so bad. My school is about to be the scene of a zombie attack, and there is nobody here to stop it – except me!

"Excuse me! Listen!" Miss Zomb shouts to the school. "Children, listen closely to us! We have something important to tell you! Listen to us, children!"

"Children... yes... yummy children...." says another zombie teacher.

"Today we are going to be doing a large cooking class, and I need you to follow our instructions very, very closely," Miss Zomb continues. "But there is no need to worry. We will not be cooking you. Nope. We won't be cooking you. So don't worry about anything. Don't worry at all, little children. We won't cook you. It's a cooking class. But for you. Not cooking you. We're not cooking you."

All the zombie teachers giggle with a horrendous and evil sound as Miss Zomb speaks.

"We are ready for it! Bring it in!" shouts one zombie teacher to the doors of the school hall.

At that moment, a large cooking pot full of boiling water is wheeled into the gym. It is black, old, and heavy, and large enough to fit everyone from the school inside!

"What's that?" Mia calls out. "That looks like a large cooking pot."

Good! Mia is starting to see the problem here.

"Don't be alarmed children," Miss Zomb explains. "This is not a large cooking pot. No, it's a... um... new... um... gym activity. Yes, that's it. A new gym activity. You all have to climb inside it to see how many of you can fit. Yes, it's a new gym activity called 'Climbing into a Pot.' Nothing to worry about. We will do the cooking class once we finish this gym activity."

"Oh, ok," Mia shrugs. "That sounds fine. It sounds totally normal, and like there is nothing to worry about."

No!

The entire school has fallen for the zombie trap!

I have to do something!

Fast!

My heart is beating hard as I think about what to do next.

I have to stop them!

I can't let the zombie teachers cook all the students from my school!

But there are eight zombie teachers, and I will need to defeat them all if I am to save everyone.

I can do it.

I know I can do it.

I can beat these zombies!

Slowly, I take Dad's laser gun out of my backpack.

This is it.

This is my moment to prove that I am capable of being a Super Spy.

I know I can do this!

I grip the gun tightly as I ready myself for the attack.

But...

I am too nervous to go.

How can I defeat eight zombie teachers all by myself?!

What if one catches me?

They'll eat me in front of the whole school!

Maybe I should try to call Dad again?

Yep, that is a good idea.

"Dad," I whisper on the phone so the zombie teachers can't hear me. "Dad, I'm at school, and the zombies have disguised themselves as school teachers. They are going to eat everyone. I need your help to defeat the zombies."

"What's that, Charlie?" Dad shouts down the phone. "I can't hear you. It must be a bad connection. I can't hear what you are saying!"

"I said that I have found the zombies," I whisper quietly again. "They are at my school. I need your help. I need you and your Super Spy team to come here and capture them."

"What?!" he shouts again. "Don't whisper, Charlie. I can't hear you."

"I have to whisper, or the zombies will hear me," I say.

"Sorry, Charlie. I can't hear you! Call me back later when you can talk louder," Dad says, and then he hangs up!

No!

That means I am the only hope left to save the school.

Come on, Charlie.

Be brave.

Be the hero.

Chapter 6

Wednesday Assembly

Zombie Attack

I can do this.

I can save the school from the zombie teacher attack.

I have to do this.

If I don't do anything, then the zombie teachers will eat all the kids in my school. I cannot let that happen.

Gripping the laser gun tightly, I take a number of deep breaths. All I have to do is run around the gym, and battle the scariest, meanest, creepiest things I have ever seen.

Easy.

Yep, totally easy...

Or maybe not!

I am so scared, but I don't have a choice. I have to save the school!

I'm going to count myself in for the attack...

5...

4...

3...

2...

1...

Go!

Ka-zap!

Ka-zap!

With excitement racing through me, I fire shot after shot of the laser gun.

My zaps hit zombie teacher after zombie teacher, and they freeze the second my laser hits them.

Awesome!

Ka-zap!

Four zombies down.

Ka-zap.

Ka-zap.

Five zombies.

Six.

Ka-zap!

Seven frozen zombie teachers.

I have defeated them all!

Yes!

I am a hero!

A job well done. I'm so proud of myself. I have defeated seven zombie teachers!

But hang on...

There were eight zombie teachers!

There is still one zombie teacher missing!

Chapter 7

Wednesday Assembly

Zombie Attack Phase 2

Turning around in a panic, I search for the last zombie teacher in the gym.

I can't see them.

They must be hiding!

Oh no!

I thought that fighting a zombie teacher was bad, but a zombie teacher that I can't find is even worse!

Then I spot her!

Miss Zomb, my substitute teacher!

She is running behind the giant pot of boiling water, and starting to push it my way!

As she pushes, the giant pot starts to tip over.

No!

The hot water pours from the top of the pot, and it rushes towards me!

Ah!

Running to the walls of the gym, I jump to the training rope in front of me. I have never been able to climb this rope, but now is the right time to start!

I pull myself up the rope super fast as the water pours in behind me!

I feel the hot water touch my shoe!

No!

I'm about to be cooked!

Quickly, I climb out of range from the boiling water.

Phew!

That was too close!

But where is Miss Zomb now?

Looking around from the top of the rope climb, I spot Miss Zomb reaching for a javelin that is stored against the gym wall.

She takes her aim...

In a split second, I turn and fire a shot from my laser gun...

Ka-Zap!

Yes!

She is frozen!

I breathe a deep sigh of relief.

Ka-Zap!

I shoot a laser at the boiling water on the ground, and it freezes! That is so cool.

Climbing back down the gym rope to the floor, I feel really proud of myself.

All the zombie teachers are frozen, and I have defended the school.

Wow.

That feels totally cool.

Mia, the cutest girl in school, is waiting for me as I climb down the rope.

"That was super brave, Charlie," she smiles. "You must be really strong, and really courageous. I'm so proud of you. You really are a hero, Charlie."

"Um… thanks," I blush.

"I am so impressed. Like super impressed. You knew something was wrong when everyone else was running around having fun, and then you defeated all the zombie teachers. You are so brave."

"Thanks," I reply again.

That seems to be about all I can say.

"Did you want to grab a milkshake after school today?" Mia asks. "I would really like to hang out with you for a while."

"I-"

Before I can finish my response, the doors to the gym burst open!

Chapter 8

Wednesday Midday

The Clean Up

"Dad?" I question.

My Super Spy Dad has burst through the doors of the gym followed by a whole bunch of his spy co-workers.

They dance around the gym doing all sorts of weird ninja moves, looking for something to attack.

"Don't worry, son," he states in his really deep voice. "Stand back. We'll protect you from the zombies. We've located them at the school, and we're here to stop them. Just move back, and we will take care of it. There is nothing to worry about now."

"But Dad-"

"The zombies appear to have been neutralized, sir," one of the spies say to Dad. "They have been zapped with a laser gun, and are all frozen into blocks of ice. There is nothing here for us to do."

"Is your Dad a spy?" Mia whispers to me.

"Yep," I nod.

"That is *sooo* cool!!" Mia gets excited.

"Did you do this, son?" Dad asks me, referring to the frozen zombies. "Did you defeat all the zombies by yourself?"

"Yes, Dad."

"Why didn't you call me?" he asks. "I would have come straight away. You really should have called me on the phone before you tried to defeat the zombies by yourself. Anything could have gone wrong. They were very dangerous zombies."

"I... don't worry, Dad."

"I'm impressed, son," Dad places his hand on my shoulder. "These were very treacherous bad guys, and you managed to defeat them all by yourself. That is the sign of a future Super Spy. These zombies were some of the meanest bad guys we have encountered for a while."

"Thanks, Dad."

"He's my friend," Mia says to my Dad, clearly impressed with my Super Spy abilities. "And he did it all by himself. He defeated all eight zombie teachers alone. He is amazing."

"Thanks, Mia," I smile.

"I think you've done an incredible job, Charlie," Dad continues. "I think we could make a spy out of you. Why don't you come down to the spy training facility with me tomorrow?"

"Really?"

"Yes, son. I have always thought that you would follow in my footsteps and become a Super Spy. After the skills that you have shown today, I think that you have earned the right to look through our top secret agency."

I look back to Mia, and she is massively impressed.

Finally, I am one of the cool kids in the school!

"But you know what we have to do now, son. After an event like this, it is part of the Super Spy protocol."

"No, Dad!" I protest. "You can't do it now! Not after what everyone just saw me do!"

"You know we have to do it, Charlie. We don't have a choice."

"But why, Dad?"

"We can't have the children of this school having nightmares about zombie teachers for the rest of their lives. You know that we have to wipe the memories of everyone after an incident like this. It is what we do after every bad incident like this. It has to be done. It is part of our procedures."

"Yes, Dad," I sigh. "Alright."

Dad pulls the memory wiper from his pocket and turns it towards everyone in the school.

"I need everyone to look over here," he says to the students. "I am going to squirt something in your direction and then you are going to feel sleepy."

SQUIRT!

And with a light squirt of liquid, everyone's memory of today is erased.

Just like that.

It's all gone.

Dad always does this when he rescues people from evil enemies. He says that if people remembered everything that happened to them, then they would all freak out.

Mia's memory of my bravery has been wiped, which means I will not be cool at school tomorrow.

When I go to school next time, not one kid will remember the moment when I saved the school from a zombie attack.

But it's not all bad.

Tomorrow, I get to go with Dad to the awesome spy training facility...

The End

Also in the Diary of a Super Spy series:

Diary of a Super Spy: Attack of the Ninjas!

Diary of a Super Spy: A Giant Problem!

Diary of a Super Spy: Space!

Diary of a Super Spy: Evil Attack!

Diary of a Super Spy: Daylight Robbery!

Also by Peter Patrick and William Thomas:

Diary of a Ninja Spy

Diary of a Ninja Spy 2

Diary of a Ninja Spy 3

Diary of a Ninja Spy 4

Diary of a Time Spy

From the Authors

Thank you for reading 'Diary of a Super Spy.'

Like all students in 6th Grade, Charlie Chucky is having fun learning how to deal with life's ups and downs. I hope you join Charlie on his next adventure – 'Diary of a Super Spy: Attack of the Ninjas!'

Have fun!

Peter Patrick and William Thomas

Special Preview Chapter:

Diary of a Super Spy:

Attack of the Ninjas

Peter Patrick

William Thomas

Chapter 1

The Spy Agency

This place is so cool.I am in the 'International Spy Building' where my Dad works as a top-secret super spy.

He is taking me for a tour of his workplace after I saved my school from a zombie attack.

I can't believe how super cool this building is.

This building has mega-smart monkeys making milkshakes, monsters cleaning toilets and witches watching television.

I have never seen anything as mad.

Everything I do here is super secret too. I'm not allowed to tell anyone about anything that I see today, even if I want to.

I wish I could.

I wish I could tell everyone at school about this – they would think it is so cool!

My Dad is the world's best super spy and I hope I can be as cool as him one day. But I'm a long way from that now...

My name is Charlie Chucky, I'm in the sixth grade and I play soccer really badly.

This is me.

And this is my Super Spy Dad.

Dad is always in a hurry.

After he has finished his meetings with the other Super Spies, he takes me for a tour of the building and points out all the super cool stuff.

Like the talking robot that looks like a tree, the lunchroom where you can eat whatever you want, and the walls that clean themselves.

I bet Mom would like those walls.

"Son, there is someone I would like you to meet," Dad says as we walk into a scientific looking room. "This is Dr. C. Mac. He is the best scientist in the whole world. If you can think it, he can invent it."

Dad introduces me to the craziest looking man I have ever seen.

Like real crazy.

"What does the C in his name stand for?" I whisper to Dad.

"Crazy."

"Oh. That makes sense."

Dr. C. Mac takes us for a tour of all his best inventions.

"This is my latest invention," he says, "It's called a backpack. It is a pack for your back! This invention will change the world!"

"Backpacks have been invented already," I say as I hold up my backpack. "Look, I have one here."

"Oh," Dr. C. Mac looks disappointed. "So they have. Well, I'll scrap that invention then."

"How about this one!" he says as he takes me over to a pair of shoes. "Um...yep, shoes have been invented before too. Look, I have a pair on now. Actually, so do you."

Dr. C. Mac looks down at his feet and realizes that he has a pair of shoes on.

"Oh yes... Well, that was a wasted couple of weeks inventing those," he mumbles.

"Don't worry about him. He's a little crazy," Dad whispers to me.

"Ahhh..." he says as he remembers something important, "That's right! This is not just a pair of shoes. This is a pair of shoes that will give you the ability to never stop running!"

Dr. C. Mac puts the shoes on his feet and begins to run around the room.

"Look!" he shouts. "I can keep running!"

He runs laps around the office.And he keeps running...

And running...

And running...

And running...

Until – SLAM!

He runs straight into a wall.

"Ouch," he says. "They may help you run further, but they don't help you steer. I must work on that."

Dr. C. Mac picks himself up, dusts himself off and begins walking to his next invention. Dad was sure right – this guy is as crazy as a coconut.

As we follow Dr. C. Mac, I spot a movement in the corner of the room. I swing my head around to look at it, and I spot a ninja hiding in the corner.

"Dad?" I pull on Dad's arm.

"Yes son?"

"Why are there ninjas in the room?" I whisper to him.

"Ninjas? That's impossible. There are no ninjas here, son."

"Yes, there is. I saw one hiding in the corner. Look over there," I point to where I just saw one.

We both look to the corner but, the ninja is not there.

"What color was he dressed in, son?"

"Black."

"Ha!" Dad laughs out loud. "Ninja's dressed in black are some of the deadliest enemies we have here at the spy building, son. There is no way that one of the ninjas could have broken into this building. We have the best security system in the world. It would be impossible!"

"But Dad, I just saw..."

"Nope. This is an A-one, top-flight building. There are definitely no ninjas here."

As we walk around the room, I look over my shoulder and see a ninja sitting in the top corner of the ceiling, watching us...

Uh-oh.

This is bad...

Read the rest of the adventure in:

Diary of a Super Spy:

Attack of the Ninjas

Available to buy now!